WELCOME TO
PASSPORT TO READING
A beginning reader's ticket to a brand-new world!

Every book in this program is designed to build read-along and read-alone skills, level by level, through engaging and enriching stories. As the reader turns each page, he or she will become more confident with new vocabulary, sight words, and comprehension.

These PASSPORT TO READING levels will help you choose the perfect book for every reader.

READING TOGETHER
Read short words in simple sentence structures together to begin a reader's journey.

READING OUT LOUD
Encourage developing readers to sound out words in more complex stories with simple vocabulary.

READING INDEPENDENTLY
Newly independent readers gain confidence reading more complex sentences with higher word counts.

READY TO READ MORE
Readers prepare for chapter books with fewer illustrations and longer paragraphs.

This book features sight words from the educator-supported Dolch Sight Words List. This encourages the reader to recognize commonly used vocabulary words, increasing reading speed and fluency.

For more information, please visit passporttoreadingbooks.com.

Enjoy the journey!

Little, Brown and Company
Hachette Book Group
1290 Avenue of the Americas, New York, NY 10104
Visit us at LBYR.com
mylittlepony.com

First Edition: May 2018

Little, Brown and Company is a division of Hachette Book Group, Inc.
The Little, Brown name and logo are trademarks of Hachette Book Group, Inc.

The publisher is not responsible for websites (or their content) that are not owned by the publisher.

Library of Congress Control Number 2017959124

ISBNs: 978-0-316-47578-5 (pbk.), 978-0-316-47580-8 (ebook), 978-0-316-47579-2 (ebook), 978-0-316-47584-6 (ebook)

Printed in the United States of America

CW

10 9 8 7 6 5 4 3

Passport to Reading titles are leveled by independent reviewers applying the standards developed by Irene Fountas and Gay Su Pinnell in *Matching Books to Readers: Using Leveled Books in Guided Reading*, Heinemann, 1999.

Licensed By:

We Are Unicorns!

by Jennifer Fox

LITTLE, BROWN AND COMPANY
New York   Boston

Attention, My Little Pony fans!

Look for these words when you read this book.

Can you spot them all?

glow

potions

teacups

broom

Each one of us has something special that makes us different.
—Princess Twilight Sparkle

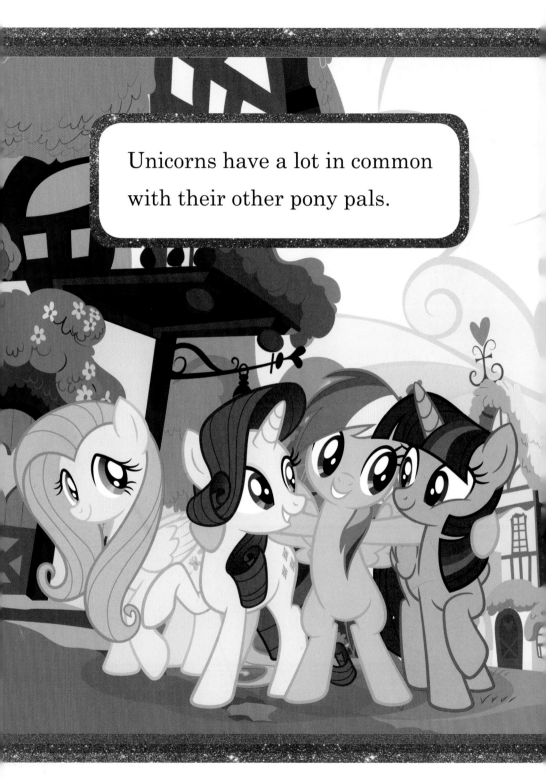

Unicorns have a lot in common with their other pony pals.

Unicorns also have something
that makes them very special...

MAGIC!

Unicorns' horns glow when
they use their magic!

Tempest's horn is broken.

She has trouble with her magic.

Her horn shoots sparks!

Magic can make you shine brightly.

Magic can help keep you
safe and sound.

Magic can also help you find
a special new friend.

Even baby Unicorns have a
little bit of magic inside of them.

They do not know how
to use it yet!

Magic is powerful.

Unicorns must learn

to use it as they grow.

They can learn how at
Princess Celestia's
School for Gifted Unicorns.

Spell books and potions
can be confusing.

Magic is not always easy
for a Unicorn to control.

"Look out!"
Trixie brews up trouble
and turns everything into teacups!
Oops!

27

Keep trying, Sweetie Belle!
Make that broom zoom.

"It is working!"

Unicorns are full of magic—
and YOU are, too.

"Look for the magic inside of you!"